Bruce
the
Brave

"For God has not given us a spirit of fear and timidity,
but of power, love, and self-discipline."
- 2 Timothy 1:7 (NLT)

Shalene C. Roberts
Illustrated by Taylor McDaniel

THIS BOOK BELONGS TO:

_____

Bruce the Brave

Shalene C. Roberts
Copyright © 2016 Shalene Roberts Creative

ISBN-13: 978-1530434930
ISBN-10: 1530434939

To Trey, our very own Bruce the Brave:

May you always know that God is with you, and He has put a spirit of power inside you. We love you!

Not so long ago, in a land not so far away, lived a little boy named Bruce the Brave. Bruce wasn't very big, in fact he was only four years old, but he was the bravest little boy you'll ever meet. At least, his daddy told him so.

Every morning as the sun peeked over the sleepy horizon, Bruce woke to a world of wonderful adventure.

Aided by his furry, four-legged sidekick, Marshall, the valiant duo were the bravest crime-fighting, hero-swaggering, treasure-hunting team you ever did see.

Together, the boy and his courageous dog unearthed the most exciting, hair-raising expeditions. Sometimes, Bruce and Marshall were a band of Jolly Buccaneers, sailing the High Seas. With swords at their sides and treasure in their sights, they steered their ship through uncharted waters, fighting off any old swashbucklin', sour-faced pirates who dared try to commandeer their ship.

Other times Bruce the Brave was a look-fear-in-the-face firefighter. When the alarm sounded, he and Marshall would make a mad dash to their at-the-ready fire truck. With sirens blazing, they would weave the truck through crowded streets in a race against time to extinguish the raging flames. Often he would even scale a treacherous ladder to reach a poor soul in need of rescuing.

There were also days when Bruce the Brave was a medieval knight. Sworn to protect the noble king and his loyal people, Bruce would ride throughout the land with a gleaming shield at his side and a helmet atop his head. If he ever confronted a band of up-to-no-gooders, Bruce and Marshall would fight so courageously that those pesky no-gooders would flee the kingdom forever, never to be seen or heard from ever again.

There were even times when Bruce and Marshall were rough-and-tumble Wild West cowboys. Astride his faithful horse, Bruce the Brave would ride the range, driving cattle down a winding, dusty trail. And as the day ended and the sun set, Marshall and he would rest beside a crackling campfire, listening to coyotes and watching his ten-gallon hat cast lengthy shadows on the ground.

Yes indeed, Bruce was certainly the bravest four-year-old in all the land, or at least in all his wide neighborhood. Nothing could frighten him …

not pirates,
nor sky-high heights,
not medieval robbers,
nor dark Wild West nights.

Each evening, after his mom and dad had tucked him into bed and Bruce had said his prayers, his dad would say, "Bruce, you are the bravest little boy I know. Now sleep well, Brave One." And away to Dreamland little Bruce would drift while dreaming of courageous acts and valiant rescues.

One night, though, when all was dark and Bruce was sound asleep, a storm rolled in with pelting rain, clattering thunder, and flashing lightning. With a loud *BOOM*, Bruce awoke in his bed with a start. As the thunder crashed and the lightning flashed, he sunk beneath his sheets. And then all the sudden, little Bruce didn't feel so brave. In fact, Bruce the Brave was absolutely, wholeheartedly, completely …

SCARED!

As the thunder crashed, little Bruce dove beneath his covers, and with his valiant bravery melting away, he quietly started to cry. But quick as the lightning flashing outside, his parents were beside his bed.

"Bruce, what's wrong?" his dad asked.

"I'm ... I'm scared," he whimpered.

Gently, his mom pulled the covers back and swept Bruce into her arms. "It's OK," she soothed. "We all get scared sometimes."

"But I'm Bruce the Brave," he cried. "Daddy told me so."

"That's right," his dad said. "You are Bruce the Brave. But being Bruce the Brave doesn't mean you won't be scared. Everyone gets scared sometimes. *What makes you brave isn't who you are but WHOSE you are.*"

"What do you mean, Daddy?" Bruce asked.

"You're a child of God, and he has given you a *spirit of power*, not a spirit of fear. You don't have to find the courage to be brave by yourself, because being brave isn't something you do. Instead, bravery is a gift given to you by the God who promises to protect you. So next time you feel scared, say a prayer. And remember ...

You're not brave because you're Bruce. You're brave because you're His."

Bruce the Brave smiled and hugged his dad tightly. He crawled back beneath the covers as his mom tucked the sheets around him. Then he snuggled next to Marshall. And as the thunder crashed, he closed his eyes, but not before whispering a brave little prayer.

"So do not fear, for I am with you."
- Isaiah 41:10 (NIV)

Now it's your turn ... Use these pages to share your own story. What causes you to be scared, and how can you trust God to make you brave?

FOLLOW ALONG

Share your Bruce the Brave moments with **#BruceTheBraveBook**

About the Author

Shalene Roberts is a grace-clinger, wife, full-time mother to four, writer, and blogger. Prior to her induction into motherhood, she was a national magazine editor. A story-teller and beauty seeker, Shalene writes with transparent honesty and authenticity about faith, family, and motherhood. Her popular post, "When Mothering is Hard and No One Sees" boasts more than half-a-million views and has been shared around the globe. She aspires to equip women to anchor in Christ, nurture grace-filled families, and foster life-giving homes. Although she currently blogs at FaithAndComposition, be sure to watch for her new site, ShaleneRoberts.com, coming soon!

Made in the USA
Lexington, KY
11 April 2016